OCT -- 2011

JE REMKIEWICZ
Remkiewicz, Frank.
Gus gets scared /

P9-EDN-446

10 | X 9/2)

WITHDRAWN

Gus
Gets
Scared

Gus
Gets
Scared

SCHOLASTIC READER
LEVEL PRE **1**
30-100 WORDS

Alameda Free Library
1550 Oak Street

by Frank Remkiewicz

Cartwheel
·B·O·O·K·S·®

SCHOLASTIC INC.
New York   Toronto   London   Auckland
Sydney   Mexico City   New Delhi   Hong Kong

For any kids who have spent
a whole night in a tent

No part of this publication may be reproduced, stored in a retrieval system, or transmitted in any form or by any means, electronic, mechanical, photocopying, recording, or otherwise, without written permission of the publisher. For information regarding permission, write to Scholastic Inc., Attention: Permissions Department, 557 Broadway, New York, NY 10012.

Copyright © 2010 by Frank Remkiewicz

All rights reserved. Published by Scholastic Inc.
SCHOLASTIC, CARTWHEEL BOOKS, and associated logos are
trademarks and/or registered trademarks of Scholastic Inc.
Lexile is a registered trademark of MetaMetrics, Inc.

Library of Congress Cataloging-in-Publication Data is available.

ISBN 978-0-545-24471-8

12 11 10 9 8 7 6 5 4   10 11 12 13 14 15/0

Printed in the U.S.A.   40
First printing, October 2010

Gus has a new tent.

"Come out," calls Mom.

Gus says no.

Gus gets toys.

Gus plays all day.

Soon it gets dark.

And cold.

Gus will sleep here.

"You are brave," says Dad.

"Very brave," says Mom.

It is dark outside.

It is dark inside.

"Come out, Dad."

What is that sound?

Gus gets scared.

"Hi, Mom."

"Good night, Mom."

Here comes the sun.

ALAMEDA FREE LIBRARY